my many emotions

Anxiety

Cherry Lake Press

Published in the United States of America by Cherry Lake Publishing Group
Ann Arbor, Michigan
www.cherrylakepublishing.com

Reading Adviser: Beth Walker Gambro, MS, Ed., Reading Consultant, Yorkville, IL
Content Adviser: Emily Fragapane, M.Ed., Ed.S., Nationally Certified School Psychologist, RYT200
Book Designer: Jennifer Wahi
Illustrator: Jeff Bane

Photo Credits: © Krakenimages.com/Shutterstock.com, 5, 7, 13; © Africa Studio/Shutterstock.com, 9; © fizkes/Shutterstock.com, 11; © Mallika Home Studio/Shutterstock.com, 15; © airdone/Shutterstock.com, 17; © Yuliya Evstratenko/Shutterstock.com, 19; © KlingSup/Shutterstock.com, 21; © TommyStockProject/Shutterstock.com, 23; Cover, 2-3, 6, 12, 22, 24, Jeff Bane

Cherry Lake Press is an imprint of Cherry Lake Publishing Group.

Library of Congress Cataloging-in-Publication Data

Names: Devera, Czeena, author. | Bane, Jeff, 1957- illustrator.
Title: Anxiety / by Czeena Devera ; illustrated by Jeff Bane.
Description: Ann Arbor, Michigan : Cherry Lake Publishing, [2021] | Series: My many emotions | Includes index. | Audience: Grades K-1
Identifiers: LCCN 2021004935 (print) | LCCN 2021004936 (ebook) | ISBN 9781534186989 (hardcover) | ISBN 9781534188389 (paperback) | ISBN 9781534189782 (pdf) | ISBN 9781534191181 (ebook)
Subjects: LCSH: Anxiety--Juvenile literature. | Emotional intelligence--Juvenile literature. | Social learning--Juvenile literature.
Classification: LCC BF575.A6 D49 2021 (print) | LCC BF575.A6 (ebook) | DDC 152.4/6--dc23
LC record available at https://lccn.loc.gov/2021004935
LC ebook record available at https://lccn.loc.gov/2021004936

Printed in the United States of America
Corporate Graphics

table of contents

About the author: Czeena Devera grew up in the red-hot heat of Arizona surrounded by books. Her childhood bedroom had built-in bookshelves that were always full. She now lives in Michigan with an even bigger library of books.

About the illustrator: Jeff Bane and his two business partners own a studio along the American River in Folsom, California, home of the 1849 Gold Rush. When Jeff's not sketching or illustrating for clients, he's either swimming or kayaking in the river to relax.

Sometimes, you might feel **Anxiety**. It can feel like questions buzzing in your head.

How would you describe Anxiety?

Anxiety can be loud. It can fill your head. It can also be sneaky. It can show up even when you don't expect it.

Anxiety can come at school. You might have forgotten your lunch. Or you’re **worried** about where to sit.

Anxiety can come with new things. Maybe you're meeting someone new. Or you're staying at a friend's house for the first time.

How does Anxiety feel to you?

Anxiety might make you feel **breathless**. Your heart might beat really fast. You might feel sick.

These are all normal **reactions**. Your body is trying to protect you. But there are things you can do to help control it.

Focus on your breathing. Count your breaths. Breathe in through your nose . . . one . . . two . . . three. Breathe out through your mouth . . . one . . . two . . . three.

Breathe in. **Imagine** smelling a flower. Breathe out. Imagine blowing out a candle.

Try exercising. **Yoga** is a great way to practice **mindfulness**.

How do you
show Anxiety?

Remember, everyone has Anxiety. Know that it won't last forever. It will come and go.

glossary & index

glossary

anxiety (ang-ZYE-uh-tee) fear or nervousness about what might happen

breathless (BRETH-liss) out of breath

imagine (i-MAJ-uhn) to picture something in your mind

mindfulness (MIND-fuhl-nuhs) being aware of your thoughts and emotions in any moment

reactions (ree-AK-shuhns) behaviors or responses to something

worried (WUHR-eed) thinking about problems or fears

yoga (YOH-guh) an exercise system that helps people relax and become physically fit

index